Oh!
For the Wings
of a Dove

Oh!
For the Wings of a Dove

A Novella

SAM NORMAN

MILO BOOKS

First published in Great Britain in November 2011
by Milo Books.

© Sam Norman 2011. All rights reserved.

ISBN 978-0-9570963-0-1

Designed by Soapbox, www.soapbox.co.uk
Printed by CPI Antony Rowe, www.cpibooks.co.uk

And I said, "Oh! For the wings of a dove!
I would fly away and be at rest.
I would flee far away
and stay in the desert;
I would hurry to my place of shelter,
far from the tempest and storm … "

PSALM 55, VV. 6-8

Chapter 1

WHEN I SAW TITANIA BLETCHLEY for the first time, I reflected that she had the sort of body that God had fashioned simply to show off. And so, several months later, it was with a feeling not entirely unrelated to delight that I received her in my drawing room in Tite Street.

Tatty and I had first met at a garden party and she had offered me a slice of lemon cake with such daintiness and charm that I had instantly felt Cupid's merciless arrow sink deep into my heart. Since then, the winning of her hand had been the first and only entry on the list of Stanwick priorities. And it was just the other day that I had gone down on one knee, popped the question, and—after a rather protracted bout of gurgling, coughing, startled-faun-in-headlights-no-steady-girl-what-would-Boadicea-have-done-dammit-yes-ness—received an answer in the affirmative.

And so, when my betrothed was shown in by my valet, Studholme, I naturally rushed to embrace her. However, with the grace of a wing-back she dropped a shoulder, shimmied left and took up a position near the mantelpiece.

"Jasper Stanwick, kindly refrain from such vulgarity. What on earth is the point of you grinning and slobbering like an orang-utang?"

I sat down, a trifle wounded.

"I was merely pleased to see you, darling. Is there so much wrong in that?"

"Darling Japper, do try to keep up. The privacy of the home is no place for such blatant displays of affection. They should be unflinchingly reserved for the public realm."

As she said this, I saw something that jolted me out of my complacency. She wasn't wearing the ring I had given her. Where it should have been, encircling that queen among index fingers, there stood only an ugly absence. I looked back up at her, the old lemon throbbing fiercely.

"I say, Tatty … "

She raised her eyebrows.

"Aren't you going to offer me something to drink?" she said.

"Would you like some tea?" I supplied.

She sighed deeply.

"Japper, if that is the best you can do, then I think it would be best if we disposed of the cordialities at once. I have something very important to tell you."

My heart suddenly started pounding out the *basso continuo* of some African ritual music. But I affected nonchalance.

"Oh?"

"Yes," she continued, raising a gloved hand to make her point. "And I must warn you, what I have to say may hurt you."

"Oh?"

"But you must remember, Japper, that this is as painful for me as it is for you."

"Oh?"

"Do stop saying Oh?. You are not a halibut. There is nothing worse in a man than indecision."

I struggled a few seconds for a suitable response.

"Please go on," I forced out at last.

"Quite. Well, as I was saying, this is a rather distasteful business."

"What is?"

She paused for a second, lost in her thoughts. Then she recovered her senses.

"Despite what you may have perceived, Japper, this was not a visit on impulse. I have decided, or rather my mother has decided, to put our engagement on hold."

Now we Stanwicks are a gentle breed. We are perfectly content to wander along, without ambition, taking joy from the simplest of life's pleasures. However, having no natural predators we are unaccustomed to attacks, and thus unaccustomed to defend ourselves. As Tatty said these words,

I entered into a sort of stupor, and sank further into my armchair. Inside, it was not too much to say that I reeled.

"Your ... mother ..." I managed to whisper at last.

"Well, refused to sanction the engagement, at least. She wants to meet you, Japper, so as to ... well, weigh you up."

"Weigh me up ..."

"Yes. Assess you. She said that she didn't like the idea of one as vulnerable as myself being descended upon by men she did not know."

"Descended upon?"

"Or words to that effect, anyway." At this point, she sat down herself, and put her hand on my knee.

"I know it's hard for you, Japper," she said comfortingly. "It's hard for me too. I am awfully fond of you. But it's not all bad. My parents have invited you to stay for the Queen's Feather."

"The what?"

"It's a pigeon race, and they always have a big house-party. So there'll be lots of people around. But the point is that I'll be there. Together, I'm sure we can make a favourable impression on Mama."

I emitted a groan. From Tatty's previous descriptions it seemed doubtful that the old girl would take to me like a pig to the proverbial.

Tatty stood up again.

"Anyway I am sure you can find your way to Daglingworth, and even you can't miss the Manor House. The Feather starts on the 18th. My parents will expect you for a drinks party they are having on the 15th. Bring a dinner jacket. I do hope all that's convenient," she added, unnecessarily.

"It isn't."

"Can't be helped, darling" she confided, and pecking me lightly on the cheek she picked up her handbag and made for the exit.

It was a somewhat deflated Japper Stanwick that showed his former fiancée, Titania Bletchley, out of his house. As I watched that Venusian figure slink off into the horizon, it occurred to me how pointless life was.

"Studholme," I heard myself call.

"Sir?" he replied, suddenly materialising at my elbow.

"A gin and tonic, if you please."

"Certainly, sir."

"And Studholme …"

"Yes, sir?"

"In that order, if you catch my drift."

I then retired to my bedroom, seeing everything in shades of grey. Two hours later I consumed dinner silently, and without company, not really noting what I was eating. I felt like the chap who said we should stop all the clocks.

Chapter 2

But they say that time is the great healer, and it was a vastly rejuvenated Japper Stanwick who greeted his valet with a stout 'Ho!' the next morning. The day was of the finest; the Sun was blossoming in the sky, the birds were trilling, the zephyrs whispered their soft susurrus through the cool morning air. I heartily gulped down a plateful of eggs and bacon, and yesterday's worries scarcely weighed upon my mind. Indeed, the day was shaping up beautifully, until Studholme entered to announce the unexpected arrival of Miss Adelaide Hutchinson-Hines.

The sinking feeling from the previous e'en resumed. Adelaide and I had had a short-lived fling many moons ago. Nothing to speak of, really. But, nevertheless, I was struck by a sense of lingering something or other on her part, whenever I saw her. It was as if it had never quite ended, if you know what I mean. Various unexpected cards and messages, and the more-than-occasional social encounter made me think that, for Adelaide at least, the flame had not waned. And there was something about the timing of her visit now …

"Adelaide – what a lovely surprise."

"Isn't it?"

We faced each other from opposite sofas, with a certain measure of distrust.

"How are you?" I asked after a few seconds' silence.

"Well, thank you," she replied briskly. She now drew a little closer, confidingly, "Jasper, there's something I must ask you …"

"Ahh …"

"Something of huge importance."

"Ooh …"

"I have wrestled with my conscience, but I cannot it put off any longer."

I saw now that I had no choice.

"Adelaide," I said, putting my foot down. "Adelaide, I am sorry. I know how it must be for you. I understand how incredibly painful you found it when we parted. You soldier on, we meet casually from time to time, but beneath the surface the flame still flickers that—who can say when?—our fates may be re-entwined. But I have to tell you that the answer is 'no'. We had our time together, but that time has passed."

Somewhat to my surprise she threw her head back and hooted with laughter.

"Japper, you immortal ass," she gasped. "The arrogance! You just assume that anything in a dress finds you irresistible. I'm sure Dr Freud has something to say about this. You're clearly compensating for something."

I blinked, vaguely wishing that a meteor would strike London SW and change the subject.

"As anyone else would have realised," resumed Adelaide, "This is strictly business. In fact, I have a small favour to ask."

"Yes?"

"I should have been much happier to have given the responsibility to someone with a bit more grip."

"What?"

"But it is pretty straightforward, and if nothing else, it can perhaps be a learning experience for you."

Well, I mean to say. I started to draw myself up to my full height; always a hard thing to do when one is sitting down.

"I hear you're off to stay at the Bletchley household?"

"How did you know that?"

"Never mind—but thanks for confirming it. Now I need you to do something for me."

"Dammit, Adelaide, if this is about Tatty ..."

"This does not concern the present unfortunate object of your affection. She is irrelevant. No, it is her father I am interested in, or more particularly one of his pets. I want you to look after a pigeon for me."

It is not within the gift of man to foretell the future. Had I known what this seemingly harmless request would lead to, I would have doubtless thrown myself through a nearby window or taken some similar course of action. As it was, I looked at her in a slightly bemused fashion. My attitude resembled that of a prehistoric caveman towards a companion, who is trying to show him what rubbing two sticks together will do.

"Look after a pigeon?" I repeated slowly. "What, play Florence Nightingale, cluster round, administer the old hot-water bottle and all that?"

"Not exactly," her voice tinkled. "The whole thing is laughably simple. You see, you have clearly never appreciated how important your future father-in-law is. He owns the largest loft of racing pigeons in the South of England. One of them is Dart of Daglingworth, the odds-on favourite to clean up at the Feather this year."

"The Feather?"

"The Queen's Feather, ass—do try to follow. You see, that's the thing about you, Japper. You meander through life without the thought crossing your mind that there might be something outside your own blinkered vision. The Queen's Feather is the Ascot of pigeon-racing. Thousands of birds compete at it, including Sir Caractacus Bletchley's Dart of Daglingworth. And when I say 'look after his pigeon', I mean put it out of action. That bird must *not* be allowed to win."

"Why not?"

It seemed a perfectly natural question at the time, but it caused Adelaide to emit a nasty laugh.

"Honestly, Jasper, did you not take in anything while we were together? Have you never realised that Daddy is also an avid follower of the sport?"

This was a harsh analysis of the situation, since I had never been close to the patriarch of the Hutchinson-Hineses. However, I must admit that deep in the Stanhope cerebellum her words did stir a few vague memories of invitations to various pigeon gymkhanas, hastily declined.

"I'll take your word for it."

"Well he is. And the Bletchleys and the Hutchinson-Hineses have had a fierce rivalry going on since before I was born. But they have now beaten us in the Feather for the last six years running, and the whole thing is getting embarrassing. This year, the Queen herself will be there, to start the main event. If we can only beat them this one time, our family honour will be restored! That is why you must nobble their pigeon."

Now, all this talk of diminished family honour was very moving, but there are some things upon which one must be firm. I could not condone this skulduggery, least of all play a part in it. I was going to Tatty's house in order to make a good impression. I hardly thought destroying the family pride and joy would help the situation.

"I'm sorry, Adelaide, but I won't do it. I refuse to kill the poor thing."

"Kill it?" she raised her eyebrows. "I don't want you to kill it. That would ruin the whole scheme. We want to beat the

Bletchleys, not just win the Feather. Without opposition, there can be no victory! No, I just want you to feed it a little something."

She extracted a small, unremarkable sachet of powder resembling fine brown sugar. I gave it a distant sniff.

"What is it?"

"What does it matter what it is? That's completely beside the point. Think of it is merely as *une petite poudre d'indisposition*. The pigeon that takes this will feel no lasting ill-effects. But, nevertheless, it serves as means to an end …"

I saw I must be adamantine in my resolve.

"No, I still won't do it."

Adelaide regarded me stonily.

"You won't?"

"Er, no … I mean emphatically not."

"You're quite sure about that?"

"Absolutely."

"Ah, well," she said, "I can't force you."

This took me completely by surprise. I had been expecting her to open up with all guns.

"Oh, good. Thanks Adelaide, I was afraid you might cut up a little rough. You know how it is, parents-in-law and all that."

"But I can perhaps offer a little … motivation."

"Eh?"

She gave a knowing smile. "Japper, that there are other ways of leaving an unfavourable impression on a family than by incapacitating their pride and joy."

The sinking feeling returned.

"Whatever do you mean?" I stammered.

"Oh, merely that I am sure nobody would want these falling into the wrong hands."

She extracted a large sheaf of crinkled papers from her handbag, and handed one of them to me. And, despite the passage of years, the faded ink and my lack of reading glasses, I at once realised that written upon them were words from my own fair hand. As I scanned the page, my jaw dangled lower and lower by gradual degree. I emitted a soft moan.

"You get my drift …"

"Yes, yes, yes, I get the picture," I interrupted quickly, vaguely hearing the soft, whistling sound of my self-esteem as it plummeted into the ground.

No-one expects old heads on young shoulders. And so it was that while I was with Adelaide, I wrote her a number of letters which it would not be too much to say were among the fruitiest epistles ever entrusted to Her Majesty's postal service. Before I met Tatty, not even Boreas himself could have cooled the fiery passion that I poured into the crinkled sheets of paper she held before me. There was no doubting what their effect would be on Tatty and her family; I would be out on the Stanwick ear with no questions asked.

"Got to be on my way. I'll leave the powder on the mantelpiece, shall I?" Adelaide said matter-of-factly.

I staggered back to the land of the living. It was not a pleasant journey.

She made her way to the door, and then turned.

"And Japper … I am rather fond of you, in a silly kind of way. But a last word of advice: if their pigeon beats ours in the Feather, don't think of showing your face in the Bletchley household, or ours, ever again."

Chapter 3

The days crawled by. The sachet of powder sat on the mantelpiece sneering at me, yet I dared not touch it. I could not for the life of me decide upon a course of action.

On the one hand, I could lay out the facts and throw myself on the mercy of the Bletchleys. However, for obvious reasons, not least the impression I had formed from Tatty of her mother, this option failed to attract. The whole history of the Japper-Hutchinson-Hines liaison would be laid bare.

Or alternatively I could give in to Adelaide's demands, administer the powder—goodness knows how—and pray I wouldn't get caught. In that case, of course, I had not only Tatty's father's wrath to fear, but also the long arm of the law fingering—if arms can finger—the Stanwick collar. By the end of the week, I had been reduced from a *soigné* man about town to a pale and quivering wreck.

It was thus with more than a little dread that I heard Studholme's words on that fateful June day; *"Sir, you must leave now if you are to make the 11 o'clock to Gloucestershire."* I took my case, then on an impulse grabbed the sachet from its perch and thrust it into my pocket. By the end of the train ride, the old fingernails were bitten to the skin. From the station I hailed a cab, and I soon found myself outside the looming gates of the Bletchley estate. It was only as we proceeded up the seemingly endless drive that I realised just how rich Tatty's family must be. The house itself was a great edifice of Cotswold stone, and was encircled by acres of open parkland. There was a faint sound of water somewhere in the distance. I paid the cab, and knocked at the gigantic oaken door. My collar had inflicted all the symptoms of lockjaw earlier in the day. Now it hung damp and lifeless around my neck.

"May I help you sir?" A slow drawl came from behind me, and I porpoised upwards with surprise. The speaker was a small, plump butler, carrying a silver dish. He was dressed in a white suit, and had a pinkish, ham-like face. He would have made a fine walrus.

"Oh, yes, rather," I stuttered. "Stanwick's the name, Jasper Stanwick, that is. I'm here to see Tatty – Titania, sorry – and co."

"May I see your invitation, sir?"

"My what?"

"Your invitation."

"Invitation for what?"

"The Bletchleys are hosting a garden party at present, sir, for the Lord Lieutenant. Security is tight. I am under strict instructions not to admit anyone without an invitation."

"But Tatty told me to come today; she didn't say anything about an invitation."

"Well, then, sir, I am afraid I must ask you to leave."

"But wait, I say … "

"Goodbye, sir."

"But hold on a sec. Couldn't you fetch Tatty – Titania, even – from the party and bring her over here. She'll vouch for me."

The butler looked down at me, which was odd as I had a good six inches on him.

"I think not sir. Miss Titania said that she was not to be disturbed."

"But dash it all … "

"I say, Compton, what's all the commotion?"

We both turned towards this third party. The butler instantly gave a discreet bow.

"I'm sorry, Ma'am. This, ah, gentleman claims Miss Titania invited him to stay."

"Ah, yes. You must be Jasper. We've heard so much about you. I am Pannonica Bletchley. Do come and join us at the party. Compton will put your bags away."

The words were welcoming, but the air had suddenly become very cold. Our eyes briefly met. In that instant, though I cannot explain it, I felt a surge of fear rise up in my throat. Every primal instinct in my body screamed out at me to drop my bags and run. I felt like a Canadian backwoodsman confronted by a grizzly bear sporting that oh-goody-lunch-at-last look. It took every ounce of logic and common sense to keep my feet fastened to the ground, and even then my knees shook a little.

"How do you do?" I spluttered out at last. There was no answer. Compton, the butler, had somehow melted away into the scenery.

Lady Bletchley had marched off before I could breathe again, but her after-image remained vividly in mind. She was tall and thin, and wore a long purple dress with a creamy white cord around her middle. On her head was perched an enormous cream hat with feathers, which leered down like a vulture. Around her neck was a cluster of sapphires and diamonds, and she wore white gloves. One could see at a glance that she was not, by nature, one of that posse of middle-aged county women who gossip about how their tulips are coming on, and give each other unwanted advice on marital matters. On the contrary, she exuded an air of raw authority. Her face was handsome, with a fine jawline; her lips seemed always to be pursed; but her eyes could make an infant wail in fear and cling to its mother's leg from fifty yards.

Compton abruptly reappeared.

"Will you follow me, sir?" he drawled, as if he found my existence no small cause for comment, before walking off around the house. We came into a large garden, in which some two hundred well-dressed people stood chatting to each other, eating cake and canapés and adjusting their monocles. A Brandy Alexander was thrust into my hand. I took a sip and instantly felt rather nauseous. When I spied Tatty in the far corner I lost no time in striding over, with the air of one stranded in the desert who has just seen an oasis.

"Darling!" she exclaimed, seeing me, and ran over and wrapped her arms around my neck. I seemed to be back in favour. She looked quite beautiful in the evening sun, and was teeming with questions. "Did you pack enough clothes? Have you met Mama? You look thinner; are you eating enough? How was your journey?"

I raised a haggard hand. "I'm not feeling too well, as it happens. What I would love is some sleep."

"Oh don't be ridiculous; you've only just arrived. There are so many people I want you to meet … "

Without waiting for a reply, she grabbed hold of my sleeve and steered me through a labyrinth of bodies.

"Now you'll be in the Blue Room, which can get a little cold at night, I'm afraid, but I'm sure you'll find it quite com… hello Alice, darling!" And I was swallowed up by the crowd.

An hour later the atmosphere was thicker than ever with drink and condescension. Nonetheless I had the impression that my every word was being quietly noted by all present. They were, so to say, kicking the tyres.

"So – Japper, you say? – what affiliation do you hold with the Bletchleys?" asked a young, heavily moustachioed man, rather coolly.

"I'm, er, or rather I was …, er, I am an old friend of Tatty," I replied, preferring to remain incognito.

"Titania?" A stout woman, in whom the first flush of youth had dulled to a light grey, addressed the wider audience in stentorian tones. "Lovely girl. Did I hear she had got engaged? I expect it's to that Travers boy, the frightfully sporty one. Yes, I distinctly remember them playing mixed doubles in the Gloucestershire Invitational last month. Tremendous match, in all senses of the word."

I found this comment markedly less funny than everyone else in the group, and I instinctively swilled down the rest of my drink. This was a mistake. Most cocktails possess their unnatural colour because of food dyes. Mine came from the vicious chemical interactions of its contents, which began to wreak havoc in the gastro-regions. While it gave me the momentary advantage of not having to think of some small talk, it tasted so strange that I very nearly gagged. With everyone looking at me, I opened my mouth to say something. Tatty, with perfect timing, emerged and pushed a huge wodge of cake into it.

But "pushed" is a hopeless euphemism. She stuffed it down my throat, like a taxidermist with a sideline in foie gras. The slice she inserted was gigantic. It was enormous. Some of it almost came out of my nose. And right at that moment some fellow clapped me on the back, causing me to inhale cake crumbs sharply. I couldn't speak, I couldn't swallow, I couldn't breathe …

"Japper, sweet one, are you all right?"

I made a low, gurgling sound in the negative. My face was becoming a very brilliant strain of pink.

"Spit it out darling, spit it out … "

Tatty's voice had disappeared far away into the background. Like the creature in *Alien*, the cocktail had bided its time. Now it prepared to make its reappearance.

"Oh my God, I think he's going to faint … "

These were the last words I heard before a tidal wave of cake crumbs and a kind of indeterminate yellow gloop erupted from my mouth. I jack-knifed forwards, unable to control myself, and took several deep breaths. I was so relieved at being able to breathe that I just kneeled on the ground, enjoying the crisp, fresh air.

Everyone had suddenly become very quiet. I stood up, and turned around.

"Enjoying the cake, I see," said Lady Pannonica Bletchley calmly, her bosom spattered with bits of marzipan and yellow streaks of vomit.

Chapter 4

It was a distinctly groggy Stanwick who was wrenched unwillingly from the land of Lethe on the following morning.

"Welcome back", said Tatty, entering my boudoir and throwing open the curtains. I groaned weakly.

"Do stop complaining," she said, matter-of-factly. "It's not as if you were the one who had to stop the party, call an ambulance, and then hoist a twelve-stone man up three flights of stairs. Mama was not pleased, to say the least. Lady Filchester fainted. We had to bring out the emergency smelling salts."

I struggled to register my apologies.

"And I must say, Japper," she continued, slightly more sharply, "I do think it was rather poor form to turn up drunk."

I sat straight up, ignoring my pain.

"What!"

"Don't deny it, Japper. You were absolutely bladdered. Positively sozzled. Everyone could see it when you came in."

I opened my mouth to rebut this appalling suggestion, but as I did so Compton seeped in at the door. For a moment, he eyed me with uncloaked distaste before saying, "Lady Bletchley has asked me to ascertain if you will be joining the family for breakfast in a quarter of an hour."

"Oh, capital, capital ... capital," I said. "The dining room, I take it?"

He regarded me, in cold assessment.

"No, sir. The Dining Room is for dining, sir. Breakfast is taken in the Breakfast Room," he said, before bowing and leaving. We watched him go.

"I'll leave you to it, Japper," resumed Tatty quickly. "Do try to buck up; we need you on good form for my mother. Oh, and a word of advice: if you have any supportive undergarments handy, I'd fish them out."

And on that slightly disturbing note, she swept out.

I dressed rapidly and made my way downstairs in haste. But outside the Breakfast Room door, calmer counsels prevailed. Okay, so my opening moves had not been an unmitigated success. But this was a long game, I told myself. Plenty of time to ingratiate myself with the Bletchleys before the moment came to depart. And so it was with spirits raised that I knocked on the door, precisely fourteen and a half minutes after the invitation had been issued, and went in.

"Mr Stanwick," I heard Compton drawl unnecessarily, by way of introduction.

"Oh, erm … What ho!"

"Good morning," replied Lady Pannonica coolly. It was not hard to see that some fence-building was in order.

"Lady Pannonica, I must apologise for last night. I can't think what came over me."

"Or me."

There seemed no answer to this, so I shuffled over and took a seat at the table. At this point, a short, balding man with a vast and very white moustache came in and tottered over.

"My dear boy, you must be St. Anwick! Charmed, I'm sure,"

"Stanwick actually,"

"Capital, capital. The name's Caractacus, by the way, Caractacus Bletchley; but you may call me Caractacus,"

"And you must call me Japper,"

"Damned gallant of you, sir. Yes, I like it when I can be frank with a man. Pains one to see all the formality that one must endure these days, wouldn't you say?"

There was a pause, and he beamed at me; his pudgy cheeks glowed with happiness and he spoke as gustily as someone fifty years his junior.

"Yes, I must say I enjoyed your performance yesterday. In fact it reminds me of when I myself was a young scallywag – like you, I was often hog-wimperingly drunk – yes,

I vividly recall one evening up at the university, when I tried to climb – now, er, what happened, let me see – oh yes, I … " he paused and scratched his forehead, unhindered in this action by any abundance of hair.

"Oh drat, the memory evades me," he concluded at last. "Anyway, it involved a violin. And soft cheese … Never mind, never mind. That's the price of age, don't you know – well I don't suppose you do, a young whippersnapper like yourself. It's a terrible thing, old age. Take my advice, St. Anwick: be while you can."

Now, I am no connoisseur of small talk, and had, I thought, been doing rather well under the circumstances. But I must admit this last comment eluded me. The conversation seemed to have taken a post-modern turn.

"Be what?"

He threw open his arms with great force, striking another guest just below the right kidney.

"You must decide that for yourself. Be! Be! Live life to the full. The world is your lobster! Was that Cicero? I think it was one of that crowd. Throw parties, go mad, steal something, play golf! You must be! I tell you, m'lad, when grey speckles your hair – that was rather good, did anyone hear that? When grey speckles your hair, I must write that down somewhere – anyway, when grey speckles your hair, m'boy, and the old hips pay their dues, then you will find yourself living out the rest of your life wondering what might have been … "

"I think that's quite enough, Caractacus," said Lady Pannonica acidly. "Mr Stanwick hasn't even been offered a cup of coffee yet."

The sage nodded his head ruefully.

"Of course, you're quite right darling. Who wants an old duffer like me lecturing them about life?"

This rang surprisingly true. The silence that ensued was so heavy that it might have been a Scottish soufflé. But presently, the enormous moustache blew upwards, the brow cleared and suddenly he was his robust self once more, shaking everyone's hand for no reason and moving smartly to the sidetable on which an array of dishes lay heaped with breakfast. "Now then, who's for a kipper?"

After the servants took away our plates, the other guests cleared off. But old man Bletchley and I were content just to sit there, honouring the meal with our silence. For this had been a breakfast unlike any other, a four-movement symphony of spectacular nourishment. The *rognons de veau caramélisés au jus* had been a particular highlight, and it was only after a third pot of coffee that the sense of bliss abated enough for either of us to able to speak.

"That ..." Sir Caractacus said slowly, savouring his words, "was a *bloody* fine breakfast."

I could not find it in me to reply. It was a *'Be still in the presence of the Lord'* moment.

"Yes," he continued. "That was simply poetry. Poetry, I tell you."

"Poetry ..." I forced out in agreement.

"Poetry," he insisted.

I sat up a little, to the extent that anyone thus stuffed to the gills can move at all.

"Yes."

There was a further pause.

"Poetry," Sir Caractacus resumed, neatly sustaining the conversation. He leant over and whispered in my ear, "It's so good to be with someone who really appreciates the good things in life. It is my experience that the female taste buds are rarely as developed as our own."

I simply nodded. Again, we sat back in silence.

"Poetry!" the knight said yet again, once more drawing on his leitmotif for inspiration.

The prosaic form of Lady Pannonica now re-entered. "That will do, Caractacus. Mr Stanwick, I understand from Titania that you are a keen rider?"

"Er ... yes."

"Excellent. I have arranged for you both to go out on a short hack after lunch."

Sir Caractacus and I looked at each other, with a mute and mutual sense of paradise lost. But we had formed a bond.

In saying I was a keen rider, mine had not been a policy of absolutely full and frank disclosure. I had had riding lessons, many of them, in childhood. Their effect had been to breed in me a healthy dislike for the horse as such, unaccompanied by any measurable degree of competence as a rider. We Stanwicks are creatures with – how can I put it? – exceptionally well-developed nervous systems. We are not among life's great supermen. Our philosophy concerning animals bigger than self is one of 'live and let live'; others might say that we possess low pain thresholds. So it was with a certain sense of foreboding that I followed Tatty after lunch towards the stables. The meaning of her cryptic remark about undergarments had become all too clear.

To all who have ever suffered Cupid's sting, I say this: you will know that surge of joy that almost bursts your heart open when you see the love of your life. But take it from me; the best antidote to this is a day out with her on the gee-gees. Repulsive creatures. As soon as they heard the faint crunch of straw under foot, six or seven of the big brutes now stuck their noses out from their respective stables, as if to enquire as to the cause of their awakening. The look, in my case, was one of undisguised disdain. Two of them had been saddled up. Without the tiniest hint of apprehension, Tatty grabbed one, inserted foot into stirrup and hopped on.

I shot a sideways glance at the horse that remained. It was a magnificent black creature about eight feet high with pointed ears and flaring nostrils, of the name of Brutus. After a few minutes of feverish endeavour to get on the animal's back – while Tatty giggled and the creature rested a scornful gaze on me, as if to say 'not *another* one' – I finally succeeded in collapsing onto the leather saddle. I looked down, only to be seized by the most terrible vertigo. The ground looked a long way away.

"Heels down, chest out, toes up," trilled Tatty.

"Yes, thank you," I replied irritably, vaguely recalling that the best strategy in an emergency was to clutch at the animal's mane.

"Heels down!" she insisted. I did my best to oblige. "Okay then, let's go," she continued, after an inspection, before giving her mount a prod and setting off.

Upon reflection, I realise that my horse could not have been going faster than an easy trot at best. But, as we came down the moss-dappled path, my only thought was that I needed to take out a hefty insurance policy against the brutes at the first available opportunity. The leather sides of the saddle were rubbing the insides of my legs raw, and the old groinal areas were coming out second best against the pommel, undergarments notwithstanding.

"Come on, Japper, *do* try to rise to the trot," I heard Tatty's voice in the distance. "After me, darling, one-two, one-two, one-two …"

Even now every one of my instincts was telling me to hurl myself off the horse's back and hope for the best. The wind was beating in my ears mercilessly. My eyes were starting to water. In the edge of my rapidly-decreasing vision, I saw Tatty give her own horse a sharp tap on the shoulder with her whip. Obligingly, it upped its gait into a slow canter. Not to be outdone, mine did likewise.

It was at this point that I realised to my horror that my saddle was starting to slip over.

"Darling, I don't believe you're even trying. Keep the impulsion, feel a contact with the horse's mouth, and *do* try to hold the reins properly. Imagine you're holding a cup of tea in each hand …"

By now, I was draped lengthways along the creature's spine. Feeling a more intimate acquaintance with the path was about to take place, I put my hands out and around the horse's neck. Its ears instantly pricked up and, freed of the rein, it moved into a highly antisocial gallop. The pommel jabbed viciously upwards, into my lower abdomen. My yelps of pain only seemed to encourage the beast.

"Jasper, now listen to me!" Tatty's voice echoed some way behind me. "Sit up and pull on the reins. Keep your back straight. One should be able to draw a line perpendicular to the ground that travels through your hands, knees and toes!"

Sadly, I caught no more of her instructions. But Brutus evidently did. Perhaps perturbed about the straightness of its back—or it may have been the perpendicularity of the line through my hands, knees and toes—the horse abruptly decided to halt. There was a faint whistling sound as man and beast parted company, in a manoeuvre technically known as an informal dismount.

I came to earth. Instantly, all the breath was knocked out of me. I made a few attempts at inhaling, before giving up and simply lying there. Every single one of my muscles was aching. I couldn't see anything in focus; it was as if I was looking at the world through a pair of very thick spectacles.

The horse peered down at me to satisfy itself that I really was injured, before losing interest and grazing quietly beside me. In spite of the blinding agony I was experiencing aside, it was a rather peaceful moment. In time, however, Tatty trotted along, and beamed down at me.

"Oh Japper, you are an immortal chump," she said, perhaps in an attempt to console me.

"If you slump down over his body like that, of course he's going to be frightened. You've got to keep your heels down. Anyway, you simply must get back on immediately. Remember the golden rule: never let a horse think you're beaten."

I emitted a faint moan. Looking at the animal, I could see it already knew.

Chapter 5

Somehow I made it back onto the horse, back to the Manor and back into bed for a nap. And it was then, after tired nature's sweet restorer had done its accustomed work and I was in the bath reassembling my various limbs into something like the right order, that I was able to review the progress of my stay thus far.

It was, I reflected, a mixed picture. On the debit side, I had thrown up on my hostess and nearly broken my back on a horse. But on the credit side, I had found something of a soul-mate in Sir Caractacus; and the ties of affection had only grown stronger with his discovery that I took an interest in pigeons. The incident occurred over lunch:

CARACTACUS:	Can I offer you some of this exquisite *faisan aux girolles en beurre satinées*?
SELF:	Oh, all right. Just a smidgen.
CARACTACUS:	I say, did you say pigeon?

SELF:	*Smid*gen.
CARACTACUS:	Because, as you know I happen to be something of a pigeon man myself. We're in the last stages of preparation for the Feather. I must take you round to meet Murgatroyd. How long have you kept pigeons?
SELF:	No, there's been a misunderstanding …
CARACTACUS:	Splendid, I didn't think so either.

Lady Pannonica, however, was an entirely different Fischwasserkessel. On the surface she remained the cordial hostess, but I was seized by a feeling of unease every time we were in the same room. Supposedly, she was weighing me up. And yet I could not help feeling that she had made her mind up already. As witness the conversation we had after I returned from the ride.

SELF:	Er … hello.
BLETCHLEY:	You had a pleasant ride, I trust.
SELF:	Oh, yes, yes. Took something of a tumble.
BLETCHLEY:	So I gather. I hope Brutus was not injured.

You see what I mean? Nice enough at first glance, but with a bit of nasty spin and lift at the end.

And so, before dinner that evening, I becollared myself resolutely. I was determined to make a good impression once and for all. "Tut, Stanwick," I said, "tut. None of this pessimistic mooching around. Remember the golden rules: one, mouth shut; two, a firm lid on the hard stuff; and three, eternal vigilance as to possible threats from La Bletchley."

It was to be another substantial gathering, and it was not long before Compton sidled into my room to ask if I would be so kind as to join everyone in the smoking room, *before* the meal was served. As I walked downstairs, I felt a little braced. Life had dealt me a good smack on the jaw, indeed two smacks, but I had taken them like a man. What else could it have to offer?

I had been under the impression that dinner would be a fairly formal affair with the local pigeon-owners in celebration of the Feather, but under closer scrutiny I found that those in question were all members of Tatty's family. They were as strange a gaggle as I had come across.

Sir Caractacus introduced me to the multitude. "Ah, everyone, this is Japper. He's a pigeon man. More sherry?"

At these words, the room came back to life, and I found myself absorbed by this innermost circle of the Bletchley clan. The sherry in question was not in fact sherry, but rather an 1847 Brandy de Jerez, served in an enormous cut-glass decanter of obvious antiquity. It was plied and re-plied. My spirits found their wings once more, and soon I had forgotten my worries.

A small, portly gentleman with a white beard came up and shook my hand enthusiastically.

"What ho, up there. Stanwick, isn't it?"

"The name's Japper."

"Auberon, actually. Auberon, Lord Duxworth. But you can call me Quacky. Titania's uncle, don't you know."

The hideous prospect of further conversation with Quacky was thankfully cut off by the dinner gong.

The meal proceeded apace, with one superb course succeeding another, and my three rules were holding fast despite an onslaught of good wine. Near the end the men started to compete with each other in telling loud and rather ribald stories.

"And then the first fellow says, *"Why not?"*" said an entirely bald man who proved to be yet another kind of cousin, at which the room erupted in laughter.

I must say, I didn't think the gag as good as all that. It wasn't a patch on the one about the three pilots. I found myself tiring of this game, and yet wanting to compete. Rule two started to waver.

"I say," I said loudly. Perhaps I was a little tipsy. "I've got a good one ..."

The room had fallen quiet.

"Right, so there's this Irishman on a train," I said. "And the lady – waitress, whatever – comes up and she says, *'Can I get you a drink?'* And the Irishman – let's call him Pat; a good Irish name, Pat – he says, *'Faith and begorrah, I'll have a whiskey.'* And the waitress gives it him, and then turns to the man next to him, who's called Mike and is a priest, and asks the same thing. And Mike says *'I would rather be ravaged by a thousand whores than allow a single drop of the demon drink to pass my lips.'*

"And then Pat, he says … he says … "

I broke off at this juncture, for I was not getting a warm feeling from the audience. My heart started pumping at approximately three times its normal rate.

"Whaddideesay?" said a lady to my right, and it seemed to me that her voice had a distinctly Irish ring to it.

"He … er … he … "

"Pray do go on," said a man at the end, who I now noticed to my horror was wearing a dog collar.

I looked round the room desperately, searching for some way of getting out of it. No way presented itself.

"Yeeeees?"

I took a deep breath.

"So Pat says, *"Oh dammit, I didn't realise there was a choice.""*

My voice tailed off until, at the end, it was only a soft tremolo. Nothing happened. I looked up, fearing the worst. There was dead silence. I had broken into a cold sweat, and fidgeted with my tie.

"Shall we move into the drawing room for coffee?" said Lady Pannonica.

We shuffled next door. But worse, much worse, was to follow. After coffee had been served a sharp clearing of the throat could be heard, the artificial cough that only occurs when someone desires to have the floor.

"Thank you," said Lady Pannonica, smiling sweetly. "It is our pleasure to welcome Mr Stanwick to Daglingworth, and I am sure we all enjoyed his last story. But family members may not be aware that he has recently proposed to Titania." There was an intake of breath around the room.

"Now, seeing as Mr Stanwick is here among so many family members, I wonder if we might persuade him to tell us all a little more about himself."

General grunting sounds were made in the affirmative.

"Excellent," continued the hostess, her smile growing wider all the time. "So, Mr Stanwick, how old are you?"

I was starting to panic. Above all, there was the way Lady Pannonica was smiling at me, that enigmatic curling of the lips that hinted at infinite malice.

"Twenty-eight, Lady Bletchley."

"Very well, and where do you live?"

"I have a small town house near Holland Park,"

"That area is not unfashionable at present," noted the Lady, almost sadly. "And what exactly is your profession?"

I adjusted my cuffs, a little ill at ease.

"To be perfectly frank, Lady Bletchley, I was left a certain sum of money when my great aunt died, and so, apart from writing a few magazine articles every now and then as the whim takes me, I can speak of no profession as such."

There were nods of approval among the spectators.

"Good," she nodded. "I always hold a man in higher esteem who has not sullied his name in such a manner. You are a gentleman. And your parents: what do they do?"

Despite my initial apprehension, I was now beginning to relax a little, like a racehorse finding its rhythm. My paranoia, having found no foothold, was starting to slip away, and I began to reflect that the whole 'do not judge other people' maxim was ringing true.

"My father was Governor General of Bengal, and he and my mother still reside in India."

Lady Bletchley inclined her head. Just as I was beginning to congratulate myself on handling the situation so well, however, the atmosphere suddenly became very still once again. The smile had returned.

"Well, that provided us all with a nice overview of your standing, but now, if I may, I should like to learn a little more about you personally," she relished, savouring each word. "I have always been of the opinion that a man's choices speak to his character far more than his words. Who is your tailor?"

This caught me off guard. I looked around, and saw everyone watching me with the utmost intent.

"Stanley & Simms of the Burlington Arcade," I stuttered at last. My answer provoked several disapproving coughs. The room seemed to be moving back against me.

"A little … racy, wouldn't you say?" remarked Lady Pannonica, raising an eyebrow. "I recollect once walking past their shop, and seeing in the window a suit of a most vivid vermilion. It is somewhat distressing to have the fads to which your generation seems espoused forced down one's throat like that. However, I digress. Have you ever worn a moustache?"

The question was so unexpected and seemingly pointless, and yet it felt like a knife at my throat.

"I did once, at Oxford, try a small moustache as an experiment," I replied, instantly feeling as though I had delivered the wrong response, "but it was very small, a mere will o'the wisp, as it were, the slightest of hints … "

The room waited in silence for the verdict.

"A moustache in anyone under 50—man or woman—is a mistake. A small moustache is worse: it shows a lack of moral grip. Worst of all, however, is a small moustache as an experiment. But sadly, time presses on. Do you belong to any clubs?"

The hideous truth now began to seep in. This was no friendly chat, but an inquisition. Lady Bletchley continued to smile, and her questions were innocuous on the surface. But their deeper import was clear. She had made her decision. And yet, much to my frustration, there was nothing I could do about it. I could hardly refuse to give an answer. Infuriatingly, her plan was working to perfection.

"I do not, Lady Bletchley."

"That is very bad," continued my torturess, unable to mask her rising sense of triumph. "The invariable rule should be one club for every decade after the age of 22. Finally, a question from Lord Duxworth: Who is the present captain of the English Association Football Team?"

This question at last gave me a glimmer of relief. Quacky had come to my rescue. I had played a good deal of football in my youth, and still made a point of following it.

"Why, Roy Goodall, of course," I answered, with a tone almost of gratitude. However, the second these words sprung from my lips, someone in their astonishment dropped a glass of sherry, which caused the entire room to erupt in horror.

My interrogator's eyes flashed with a malevolent pleasure. Lady Bletchley stood up, with an air of utter finality. I seemed to see a thunderhead form above her and huge lightning strikes forking downwards.

"Mr Stanwick," she declared in triumph over the hubbub, "A man's predilections are his own business, but in this household we regard football as the most vulgar of sports. Your answers have betrayed you for a man of few graces and little social distinction. You have entertained some fancy of asking for my daughter's hand in marriage. I cannot speak for her father, of course. But for myself, I should be loath to marry off our only daughter, a girl upon whom we have doted for twenty-five years, to a man who self-evidently could not even tell a runcible from a bouillon."

There was a general murmur of approbation from around the room. I stood, took my leave with as much dignity as I could muster, and made my way back to my room.

And then suddenly I understood all. This whole line of questioning had been a charade. My stay at Daglingworth had not taken place to give Lady Pannonica a good impression of me. She had made up her mind before I had even arrived at the Manor House. Scheming witch that she was, she had deliberately engineered a series of social and, yes, sporting tests—who could forget Brutus?—whose purpose had been to humiliate and embarrass me in front of the family and, worst of all, in front of Tatty. No love could survive that onslaught. And, like the Romans after the battle of Cannae, I had to admit that Lady Pannonica's plan had worked flawlessly.

Yet, there was something inside me that yearned to fight. From the second Tatty had stepped onto my hearth all those weeks ago bearing bad tidings, my heart had been heavy with anxiety and indecision. As soon as I had arrived at the Manor House, I had been greeted with the cold stare and the narrowed eye. My natural instinct was not to fight it. But now, miraculously, just at the moment of greatest crisis, my classical education showed its worth. Thousands of years ago, I recalled, the Ancient Greeks were scampering around trying to escape from the Persians, who were set on world domination or some rot like that. At one point a group of Athenians, or as it may be Spartans, needed to hold a pass, or possibly bridge. So they positioned themselves in such a way that the Persians would have no choice but to fight them. The Persians trotted up, and the two sides exchanged pleasantries such as "Our arrows will blot out the sun" and the rather banterous "Well then at least we'll have some shade to knock you off in." Finally, the Persians, who had a vastly bigger and better equipped army, delivered their ultimatum; in a nutshell, "Hand over your weapons." To which the Spartans, or as it may be Athenians, answered with the immortal "Molon labe", which translates as "Come and get them yourselves", with a large whiff of "and get stuffed."

I am not absolutely sure I have nailed the details down, but the thrust or gist of the tale was clear. So now, just when the old sinews were stretched tighter than a Welshman's wallet, something inside me was throbbing – no, positively thrilling – with the message "Enough is enough". I felt, like Henry V at Agincourt, when he was God-for-Harry-England-and-St.-Georgeing it, that the time had come to grit one's teeth, put the old foot down and shout "No more!"

The old Stanwick backbone had returned. I looked at myself in the large, ornate mirror that stood aloof on the wall, and started to think about revenge.

Chapter 6

Revenge, they say, is a dish best eaten cold; and true to form the moment of *vendetta* did not immediately present itself. Tatty was clearly avoiding me, but the same was not true of Sir Caractacus. On the contrary, he clustered round like a trooper, completely oblivious of my recent descent into social pariahdom. The reason for this was not far to seek. Tomorrow was the Queen's Feather. Having identified me as a fellow enthusiast, Sir Caractacus was keen to show off his magnificent pigeon-nurturing operation in every aspect. So the following day we were up before breakfast for an encounter with Murgatroyd, the pigeon-keeper.

Murgatroyd proved to be a beetle-browed Scot, who looked like he might have been God's sighting shot before He attempted the chimpanzee. Sir Caractacus introduced us in the pigeon loft, a suite of rooms at the top of the house so magnificent that they would not have been out of place in the Taj Mahal. The only difference, so far as I could see, was that the loft had a definite whiff, or rather an extreme stench, of pigeon-droppings; a touch which, speaking personally, I rather thought Shah Jehan would have done without.

It was evident that the pigeons did not share my view of the accommodations. Nest boxes filled the place as far as the eye could see. Dozens of birds were cooing with appreciation at the work of Murgatroyd, who moved about them with a grace surprising in one so unabashedly anthropoidal.

"Jasper St. Anwick, Hamish Murgatroyd, and naturally vice versa," said Sir Caractacus.

Murgatroyd uttered a low grunt. He did not strike me as a potential soul-mate.

"Tremendous to meet you," I gushed, offering my hand.

He eyed me. I withdrew my outstretched arm.

"Mfngkmhrhrghm," he uttered cryptically, not taking his eyes off me for an instant. His brows, which had previously beetled extensively, now redoubled their beetling. It was obvious what was going through the Murgatroyd mind, or mind-equivalent: who, pray, might this dubious newcomer be?

"My thoughts exactly, especially on the eve of the Feather", said Sir Caractacus, who had obviously mastered the Murgatroyd idiolect. "But you need have no fear. St. Anwick is a true pigeon man."

"Is that sooo?" asked the Scot softly. "Tell me, surreh, wheech particular denomination of columbology is yur speciality?"

It was a nasty moment. I opted for the flannel nonchalant.

"Well, one doesn't like to ... "

"Are ye a student of the Brereton-Shuttlewurreth system?"

"Aaah, I think it would be invidious to ascribe ... "

"Or d'ye take a more holistic approach, perhaps?"

"Oh, erm ... rather."

"How fortunate."

The reader may have formed the impression at this point that all was just gay badinage between us, but that would be a serious error. Beneath my nonchalance, I was casting a hawk-like eye at the pigeon-man and his place of work. And the more I looked at it, the more I saw the sheer impossibility of the task Adelaide had set me. I had never exactly warmed to the idea. Now I saw that it was out of the question. Which bird was Dart of Daglingworth? Where precisely did it reside? How was it fed? And, coming to the point at issue, with Murgatroyd prowling and prowling around like the proverbial troops of Midian, how on earth could the brown powder be transferred from the small sachet in my coat pocket into the bird's digestive tract?

Amid these cogitations, there was one bright spot, one safe harbour in a sea of troubles: my own digestive tract was at no risk of under-nourishment. The food at Daglingworth remained magnificent, and breakfast post-Murgatroyd was no exception. You know that a meal is right up there when a man like Sir Caractacus is content just to lie back and emit soft, whooshing sounds through the nostrils. But this breakfast was so transcendent that we did not go through the charade of praising it with mere words. It would have been blasphemy.

"Gustave … " Sir Caractacus forced out at last. "The chef … we must congratulate him … "

United by a single thought, we staggered to our feet and made our way towards the kitchen. Entering a part of the house that I had not yet explored, we arrived at a huge oval door, set a few inches off the ground. There hung around it the pleasant smell of fresh bread.

"Now, Japper m'boy," the noble knight said softly, "Gustave is perfectly tame, but you must remember: if you had spent the past thirty years of your life eating food of the richness that he has, you wouldn't be entirely sane either."

And with that, he knocked sharply and pushed open the door.

Inside, I saw a very small and very round man with a plump complexion rolling out some dough. For a moment, he squinted at us, before flinging his arms open and gushing, "*Monsieur le Caractacoo!*"

"Yes, yes," blustered the knight with the sort of uneasy amusement that one might derive from being licked by a more than usually outgoing St Bernard, as Gustave bounded over and kissed him heartily on either cheek.

"It has been too long, *monsieur*," the Frenchman continued, beaming up at Sir Caractacus.

"Well, ah, only in fact about twelve hours," Sir Caractacus managed to free himself from the Frenchman's murderous embrace, and took up a strategic position next to the back wall. Gustave continued to beam. Sir Caractacus nodded in my direction, and the Frenchman turned his head.

"Monsieur?"

"Ah, jemapple Jasper Stanwick. On-shan-tay" I said, retrieving from distant memory a formula that had served me well since prep school.

Gustave raised his eyebrows.

"*Vous êtes français? Personne ne m'a dit qu'un français était arrivé…*"

"Erm … no, or rather non," I said, before things got out of hand. "I'm, er, actually I'm English."

Gustave regarded me through narrowed eyes, as if asking himself what could have possessed me to play such a mean trick. Then his face cleared.

"*Que vous êtes charmant*," he said.

"Ah, well, now that you've got to know each other, Gustave, we'll leave you to it," said Sir Caractacus. Then his voice dropped, as he addressed the cook in a conspiratorial whisper. "By the way, have you, er, got the *you-know-what?*".

The Frenchman nodded a nod of quiet comprehension. Without a word, he brought over a large tureen and raised the lid. Sir Caractacus smiled.

"Now, Japper, old fellow", he said in hushed tones. "I know you're a pigeon man, but I bet you can't guess what this is?"

I vaguely looked. The tureen was filled with a musty-smelling beige substance.

"I couldn't say," I replied vaguely.

"Oh come on, have a guess," insisted Sir Caractacus. "It's my secret ingredient. Not a single other soul in the entire world outside this household knows."

"I haven't the foggiest …"

"Gustave's own truffle mash," the knight said triumphantly. "The truffles here at Daglingworth are simply first-rate. Our pigs sniff them out in the local woods—can't tell you where, of course, closely guarded secret. And do you know what? They enhance a pigeon's performance like nothing else. Simply brimming in vitamins and general vigour-inducing substances."

"We do take caire of our pigeons," chipped in Gustave.

"Oh yes, we even bring them their food on a silver plate," continued Sir Caractacus.

"*Non, non, monsieur*," Gustave interjected, "It is pronounced *s'il vous plait.*"

While they wrestled with the intricacies of French pronunciation, a sudden thought hit me square on the nose. *This was the pigeon feed, the feed itself, before me.* Sir Caractacus was exactly the kind of man who would insist that it be prepared specially—and by Gustave himself, no less. The secret ingredient, the supercharged buck-u-uppo that gave Dart of Daglingworth its racing edge … it all made perfect sense.

There are some times in life when a single word can change a man. It can send him into an adrenaline-fuelled frenzy, so that he is capable of superhuman achievements, or make his mind so sharp as to pick up on the slightest of unconscious messages. This was not one of those times. But the moment had come. I could feel the sachet of powder in my coat pocket, against my pounding heart.

And yet I hesitated, like the cat in the adage who let "I dare not" wait upon "I would". Who was to say what effect the powder might have? I saw Gustave holding the tureen. The sachet burned against my skin. Sir Caractacus rambled on. But I seemed to have lost connection with the rest of the world. Should I take my chances? Should I bide my time? The questions swirled around my head as never before.

Then suddenly Lady Bletchley's denunciation from the previous evening resounded in my ear like a clarion. *I should be loath to marry off our only daughter, a girl upon whom we have doted for twenty-five years, to a man who self-evidently could not even tell a runcible from a bouillon.* Hah, runcible! Pshaw, bouillon! The evil old crone. Molon labe!

I remember a friend at Oxford whose skill with cards meant he never went short of a drink. Whenever the thirst overcame him, as it regularly did, he simply went up to the bar and bet the nearest fellow a martini that he had the Queen of Spades in his shoe. One day I asked him how he did it. "It's not about the cards, Japper", he said. "It's not even about sleight of hand. You must misdirect. Put them off the scent." And lo and behold he was right. I started to notice the most amazing things. A slight relaxation of the shoulders, a flicker of eye-contact, a momentary distraction and he would make his move.

No time for all that shoulder-relaxing and eye-flickering now, however.

"I say, look over there!" I exclaimed. It sounded a little weak, but needs must.

They both glanced behind them.

"What was it? A tiger?" said Sir Caractacus, looking around him anxiously.

"Er, no … It was, well … "

And I would have babbled on in this vein, when inspiration came to me. Behind Sir Caractacus stood the enormous sherry decanter on a side table. And though most of its ambrosial contents had been swigged down, it was still about a quarter full.

"I thought I saw one of your racing pigeons lying under the table."

I never saw the expression of a man change so rapidly. I'm not sure what the world record is for Caractaci in the standing high jump, but this one was a definite contender. He gave a violent start.

"Egad, sir, all hands on deck", yodelled Sir Caractacus, spinning round—and catching the decanter a blow with his arm en route.

"Look out!" I yelled. But it was too late.

For a second the decanter teetered, as if on the edge of an abyss. And then slowly, inevitably, it toppled forward. It hit the ground, the glass shattered, and the priceless liquid shot out across the floor.

Sir Caractacus threw himself to the ground.

"*Aaaarrgghh! Not the 1847 Brandy de Jerez!*" he cried, as he made frantic efforts to scoop as much of the liquid up with his hands as he could. For his part Gustave had laid the mash down, and was instantly by the knight's side.

And there it was, in front of me.

The bowl of mash smiled up. I smiled back. Gustave and Sir Caractacus continued to scrabble away in the background. As if in slow motion, I saw myself take out the sachet of powder and look down at it. It caught the light playfully. It seemed to be daring me … *go on, do it …* I looked round. I couldn't … it was so blatant. *Runcible … bouillon …* Before I quite realised what I was doing, I had opened the little packet and sprinkled its contents onto the mash. The powder was almost instantly absorbed. Within seconds the two colours were virtually indistinguishable.

I felt a pang of disbelief at what I had just done. It was as if I had just pressed a button to create some terrific explosion somewhere, but nothing had happened. I felt weightless, unable to come to terms with the consequences of such a seemingly meaningless action.

The two men had by now got to their feet. I began to deliver profuse apologies, but Sir Caractacus waved them away. And suddenly Gustave had taken the tureen in his arms—had he noticed? No! He was walking towards a warming cupboard, was opening it, and now my secret was hidden safely on the top shelf ... I felt a surge of relief and self-congratulation, but there was no time for that. Neither of the others could be allowed to realise that anything was amiss.

"I say!" I blurted out suddenly, feeling that I had to contribute.

Both heads turned in my direction.

"Yes?", said Sir Caractacus.

I was forced to concede, at this point, that my last comment, while entirely accurate in and of itself, did not advance the conversation. I said, but I had nothing to say. My mind was a complete blank.

"Erm ... yes," I spluttered.

Sir Caractacus raised his eyebrows.

"Yes?"

"Er ... er ... truffles, you say?"

"Ah," the knight had returned to a subject close to his heart. "Yes, truffles. A superb source of bromine, which is essential for the maintenance of a good, healthy cardiovascular system ... "

I breathed a sigh of relief. I had got away with it. And yet unease gnawed my heart. What effects might the powder prove to have?

Chapter 7

Lunch was a desultory affair. Lady Bletchley had not warmed up from the previous evening, and glowered icily at me from the other side. Sir Caractacus had fallen into brief depression at the loss of his Jerez, and said nothing. Tatty sat in mute solidarity with her mother. The other guests took their cue from them.

Soon the food arrived, accompanied by an unusually bubbly Gustave. He was practically jumping out of his sandals.

"*Mesdames et Messieurs,*" he spouted. "I have a very special treat for you today ... In honour of the Queen's Feathaire tomorrow, I have reserved some of my signature truffle sauce for your lunch. It will, I think, perfectly complement the *saveur épicier* of the stuffed quails."

Sir Caractacus's moustache flew upwards.

"Excellent!" he said with renewed vigour. "That's the best news I've heard all day. Ah! Here is the food now! I can smell that magnificent odour a mile off ... "

But his words fell on deaf ears. It was a meditative Stanwick who now contemplated the full import of Gustave's words. A goodly sachet of Adelaide's powder had gone into that sauce and what, I said to myself with a biblical touch, what would be the harvest?

"I'm … I'm actually fine," I stammered, as the servant placed my meal before me. Suddenly, there was dead silence. Even the quail held its breath.

"I'm sorry?" said Sir Caractacus, disbelievingly.

"I … well, I … the truth is I am not a huge truffle man. Really, they'd be wasted on me."

This was a blunder. Instantly spotting it, Lady Bletchley tsk-tsked, then stepped aside to give her husband a clear shot. I dangled before that moustache.

"Mr Stanwick," said Sir Caractacus, very softly. "Am I to understand that you are refusing Gustave's truffle sauce?"

"Well, I … that is to say … "

"Do you not realise the lengths to which that colossal culinary titan has gone to procure such a feast? Have you any conception of the enormous expense and sacrifice involved, that we might enjoy this most simple of pleasures?"

"I … erm, well this is dashed awkward … "

"Are you insulting the name of Bletchley, sir? A name that has stood proud for nearly nine hundred years, ever since the *Vicomte de Bletchlaye* personally commanded the Norman bowmen at the Battle of Hastings?"

"Ah, well, er … "

"Do you think, sir, that when the Conqueror himself sat his army down to the victory feast on that memorable evening, he had to put up with a Bletchlaye indicating that he was a vegetarian, and asking whether he could give the roast beef the old miss-in-baulk?

"Mr Stanwick." It was Lady Bletchley who spoke this time. Sir Caractacus judiciously shut up. "Feel free to start whenever you like."

"I tell you I …"

"Jasper." This from Tatty.

"But, I can't …"

"Jasper!"

"Oh, all right then."

My decision to tuck in was not, I should hasten to make clear, the pure result either of spinelessness or a death wish. No: for a fleeting moment, my eyes met those of Lady Bletchley, and I saw something in her expression. She was willing me not to eat it. She was praying that I would refuse, cutting away any last bond or tie to Sir Caractacus. It would be, for her, the final victory.

But this time the worm would not turn, I told myself. This time there would be no compromise. This time I refused to announce unconditional surrender. And if I had to go gentle into that good night, then at least I would rage, rage, against the dying of the light. Or something.

Was it not Achilles who chose a short, glorious life over a long, insipid one? The Achillean choice comes to us all, in varying degrees. For some reason, there always seems to be a woman at the heart of things. But, in such cases, we must choose between what is easy, and what is right. The Stanwick honour had been dragged through the mire ever since my arrival, and yet it hadn't altogether lost shape. Just as Achilles put on Vulcan's armour in the knowledge that it was his destiny to die that day, so too did Stanwick gesture for Lady Bletchley to pass the truffle sauce.

"My beamish boy!" exclaimed Sir Caractacus, as he sprung to his feet, and brought it over himself. "So glad you've come round. You won't regret it, I tell you! Gustave does this little thing whereby he adds just the faintest waft of coriander …"

I glanced over at Lady Bletchley. Her face was a mask of exasperation and muffled rage.

Sir Caractacus' kindly disposition was a double-edged sword, however. Such was his bonhomie that he positively lathered my dish with the stuff. Everything was sodden with it. Still, it was designed for pigeons—how bad could it be?

"Ahhh …" I uttered, as he drowned the quail in the evil-smelling sauce. Instantly, there was once more dead silence.

"Yes, St. Anwick?" he spoke softly, in his previous tone.

"Oh … erm, nothing," I replied. The moustache elated.

"Excellent! Eat up."

The question of how bad it could be was soon answered. I finished lunch at 2.26pm and headed towards my room for a brief siesta. At 3.04pm I was seized with violent stomach cramps, at 3.06pm staggering towards the nearest lavatory at high speed, at 3.07pm taking up an entrenched position on a fine example of Sir Thomas Crapper's immortal masterwork. Close to hand was a volume entitled *British Bats: A Field Guide for the Amateur*. By 5.33pm I had become highly expert in the habits and diets of soprano pipistrelles and horseshoe bats. I had also relieved myself of a significant fraction of my body weight.

It was a drained and whitened Jasper Stanwick that limped out at around 6pm, clutching his stomach and moaning like a wounded dog. My bowels felt like they were trying to make a martini, and not caring too much whether it was shaken or stirred.

As I made my way downstairs, I came across Sir Caractacus. But this was a Sir Caractacus unlike any other. He seemed to have aged about 150 years in two hours. His face was gaunt and sweaty. Even his moustache looked tired.

"Ah Jasper, there you are, m'lad," he forced out, raising a shaky hand. His voice was hollow, almost broken. "Good to see you ... just had the most excruciating case of the runs, don't you know. Ah, but that's the price of old age."

"Diarrhoea?" I interrupted bluntly.

He raised his head, and smiled a little.

"An understatement, m'boy. An understatement. Whatever the sins visited on the ancient Incas, Montezuma has taken full and ample revenge."

That set the old bean throbbing. It seemed impossible that this could be a mere coincidence. But were the other members of the family affected, and if so how badly?

"Yes, quite, me too, so to speak," I spluttered. "Now, quickly, we must find the others …"

Sir Caractacus obligingly tottered along behind me, and before long we came across Lady Bletchley. I was pleased to see that for the first time she was not exuding sheer power. On the contrary, she looked highly uncomfortable.

"I say, darling," began the knight, "are you all right?"

Lady Bletchley looked down, guardedly.

"I've been … powdering my nose," she replied cagily.

"Powdering your nose?"

"Caractacus, do stop being so dull. I've been *powdering my nose*."

"Ah," said the peer knowingly. "You mean, powdering it on the lavatory."

"Quite so."

"Well, it just so happens that Japper and I have been doing exactly the same thing."

"But don't you see?" I ventured. "We must have all been subject to some sort of food poisoning. The truffle sauce, perhaps …"

"No, dammit!" Sir Caractacus stamped his foot in anger. "It was not the truffle sauce. I have enjoyed Gustave's truffle sauce for over twenty years and I tell you that was as fine as it's ever been!"

"Well, it hardly matters." Tatty had joined us. "Japper's right. Something in the meal was obviously a little off. We simply must call for a doctor."

Doctor Binney was sent for, and we dispersed unhappily to our rooms to await his arrival.

Chapter 8

"I'M AFRAID THERE'S NOTHING TO be done," said Dr Binney an hour later. "You all have serious cases of diarrhoea. I should say food poisoning rather than gastro-enteritis. Rest and plenty of liquids ought to do the trick. Don't want to get dehydrated. No milk or coffee."

Lady Bletchley gave him a stare that could shatter a brick.

"Dr Binney, we have to leave first thing tomorrow for a very important public event. Could you not give us something to settle our stomachs?"

"Well of course there's always milk of magnesia, Lady Bletchley. But food poisoning has many causes. It can be caused by bacteria, or a virus, or ingestion of a toxin—even a parasite. We don't want to mask the symptoms. Could get very sticky."

There was a moment's silence, as this set in.

"Well, wash me in steep-down gulfs of raspberry jam," said Sir Caractacus wearily. "And so close to the Queen's Feather."

Dr Binney nodded sympathetically. But Lady Pannonica was not to be thwarted.

"Don't be ridiculous, Caractacus! I'm not going to bow out of the Feather and hand the thing over lock, stock and barrel to those awful Hutchinson-Hines people," she exclaimed. "Doctor Binney, are you seriously telling me that you have nothing to hand which can help us to get through the next 24 hours? The matter is of vital importance."

"Lady Bletchley, there are pills of a sufficient concentration. However, they are extremely strong. Taking them is not advisable given the position in which you find yourselves."

"Well then, let us have those pills immediately!" she positively screeched. I'd never seen anything in a straw hat look so angry.

"Very well, Lady Bletchley," replied Dr Binney, with dignity. "Although I must warn you, there is a risk of constipation which could be almost as distressing as your current state. But, as you wish, I shall have a prescription made up and the pills sent over shortly."

At this point there was a quick knock at the door. It was Compton. Something about his manner was not as suave as usual.

"Sir Caractacus, Lady Bletchley," he addressed, in broken tones. "There's been an accident … in the kitchen … Monsieur Delamerdemamère …"

"Gustave!" exclaimed Sir Caractacus, imprudently jumping to his feet, then clutching his sides with the pain.

"Indeed, sir … I fear the worst …"

As one, we legged it down to the kitchen, followed by Dr Binney. Sir Caractacus flung open the door, to see the poor Frenchman bent double on the ground, with Murgatroyd clustering round. On the cook's face was a look of convulsive pain, and he was clutching at his abdominal regions. No mean achievement, given his nearly spherical shape.

"Gustave!" exclaimed Sir Caractacus, as he got down on one knee beside his chef. "Are you there? What's happened?"

The Frenchman looked up, a look of anguish on his countenance.

"*Cher Maître* … you 'eff been too good to me … I 'eff lost the *huile d'olive* …"

"Eh, *huile d'olive?* Olive oil?"

We groped around a bit over this one while Gustave groaned. Then I saw all.

"I think he means the will to live, Sir Caractacus."

"What are you talking about?" The knight was near hysterical.

"*La sauce de truffe* …" Gustave continued. "It was just too delicious …"

"What?"

Gustave reached out, flinching with the effort, and held Sir Caractacus's hand.

"*Monsieur*, over many years, when you were playing at golf, or entertaining your guests, I would secretly sneak the truffle sauce. I couldn't bear to create something so beautiful, and yet only be able to taste it. Nothing had come of it until today – and I swear, *cher Maître*, zis was to be the last time – but … well, *mon Dieu* has punished me. Please … forgive me, sir … I could neffer hurt you … "

With this, the Frenchman rolled onto his side, and passed out.

As Dr Binney supervised the transfer of Gustave into an ambulance shortly afterwards, Sir Caractacus addressed us all with an air of quiet solemnity.

"The fault is mine," he said. "I should never have thrust so great a responsibility onto the shoulders of one man. There's only so much one can take, before cracking under the pressure. Serving his culinary muse, feeding the entire household, the servants, the pigeons … "

Suddenly, he broke off, and his face blanched.

"The pigeons!" he gasped, and shot a look of horror at Murgatroyd. "Have they been fed?"

"Yes, Sirrah Caractacus, I carried it out it mysel' as normal this e'enin'. Nothing was allowed to contaminate the mash."

"But don't you see? It wasn't food-poisoning at all. The mash was contaminated! Some overseas pigeon cartel has spiked it, knowing it would be fed to my birds. It's a conspiracy," said Sir Caractacus, getting into his stride. "They've infiltrated the household."

"What are you on about, Caractacus?" asked Lady Pannonica curtly.

"They've been trying for weeks. They're after Dart of Daglingworth …"

"Who's they?"

Sir Caractacus spread his arms wide open.

"How should I know? There are any number of people who probably have an interest in my prizewinning bird not competing tomorrow. The Mafia, I shouldn't wonder. The *Union Corse*. The Yakuza, or the Mossad. Perhaps the Russian Secret Service. And tomorrow, our pigeon will barely be able to get out of its basket …"

There was silence at his words. Tatty started sobbing quiet chokes of grief. Lady Bletchley looked almost deranged.

"Is there nothing we can do? The pigeon has been poisoned. Can we not give it an antidote?" she said, hardly able to force the words out.

"Out of the question," replied Sir Caractacus. "Section 47 of the Manual of Columbology specifically states …"

"Oh, to hell with the Manual of Columbology!" interrupted Lady Bletchley, but Sir Caractacus raised a hand, white with determination.

"We *obviously* cannot feed a pigeon any kind of drug just before a race. It would be against every rule in the book. I could never show my face in public again."

"What about your precious truffle mash?" she snapped. "Is that not a drug?"

"Daglingworth truffles are naturally occurring organic substances!" Sir Caractacus cried. "Just because they happen to be so fantastically nitrogenous and vitamin-rich in their chemical make-up is no fault of mine!"

"But how do they check?" Lady Pannonica persisted, trying a different tack. "Do they subject each and every pigeon to rigorous testing?"

"Of course not!" retorted the knight. "But my dear Pannonica, as you know perfectly well, we are talking about a sport played by the noblest families in England. Nobody would ever dream of disobeying a rule like that. It would be worse than kicking the ball at croquet."

"But the Hutchinson-Hineses … " Lady Bletchley wailed, only for Sir Caractacus to give her a look of such scorching intensity that she threw in the towel.

"We may lose tomorrow," said the knight, more gently. "The glorious record of the past six years may finally perish. But I would never defile the immortal name of Bletchley by cheating in so unscrupulous a manner. Only the most blistering of blistering high-binders would ever entertain that idea for so much as an instant."

And with that final pronouncement he retired, as we all did, to bed.

Mine was not a happy night. The insides continued to churn. I lay awake fretting that the pigeon-poisoning might finally be traced back to me, or slept fitfully, beset by hideous visions of pigeons turning into vultures. It was well after midnight when I suddenly awoke for yet another call of nature. The little bathroom attached to my bedroom had long since given up the ghost, so I pulled on my dressing-gown and slippers and made for the lavatory down the corridor, which had become my home away from home.

However, to my surprise, as soon as I left the lavatory my darkness-adapted eyes instantly caught sight of a dim light, further down the corridor. Intrigued, I stole towards it. A gowned figure was holding a candle, and moving swiftly away from me. It was Lady Bletchley! I almost cried out, but managed to stop myself at the last second. Something about the way she crouched as she walked aroused my suspicions, and I followed her. Moving as silently as a cat, she stole along the full length of the corridor, and then descended down the spiral staircase. I did likewise. We turned left, moving towards the Old Wing. At one point, she glanced suddenly behind her, but the darkness was so stubborn and unyielding that it provided a convenient camouflage. With her mind at rest, she opened a door and slipped inside. It was the staircase to the pigeon loft! Again I followed her, tracking the light as it moved up the ancient stairs. She entered the loft. I climbed the stairs, then stood noiselessly behind the door, watching her every move.

Lady Bletchley had set the candle down. It cast unearthly shadows about the room, and I was conscious of hundreds of small bodies in every nest box, as the pigeons slumbered or watched us drowsily. She was searching in her dressing gown for something. Her actions were unhurried, and yet she kept casting worried glances at the doorway, as if expecting someone.

The faint light of the candle had reduced her to little more than a silhouette, but her next action was unmistakeable. From the pocket of her dressing gown, I saw her extract a bottle of tiny blue pills. Then, with the steady hand of one who knows what must be done, she reached into a nest box and held the pill towards the prize pigeon. It looked at the pill for a few seconds, cocked its head, and then nibbled at it. Then some more. And now it had ingested the whole thing, and the pill was making its way down the bird's oesophagus. Satisfied, Lady Bletchley cast another look at the pigeon, before closing the box, picking up her candle and making to leave. I felt the time had come to make my presence known, pushed open the door and flicked on the light.

I never saw such a violent change in man or woman. Temporarily blinded, she jumped about twelve feet in the air, spun round, slipped and fell over, dropping the pills. For a few seconds, she gaped up at me in disbelief.

"*Mr Stanwick!*" she cried at last. "What on earth are you doing here?"

"Rise, Lady Bletchley, from that semi-recumbent posture. It is most indecorous," I said suavely. We Stanwicks are very suave in these situations. "I might ask you the same thing."

She looked like she'd swallowed a lemon.

"I … well, I … look, this is absurd. You have no place here. Get back to your room, I tell you!"

"Well, you won't mind if I tell Sir Caractacus about our chance meeting then? Such an extraordinary coincidence … " I picked up a couple of the little blue pills.

"Yes! No, wait … I say … "

I turned back round, my hand on the door latch. She looked at me imploringly.

"You don't understand. This is the only option … "

"Drugging your pigeon, so as to win a race?"

"You have no idea what it's like … the pressure. Everyone will be watching tomorrow. The Queen will be there! If that pigeon fails, we will be a laughing stock."

"But constipation pills?"

"They're the only shot we have!" she practically screamed.

It suddenly struck me that I was in a position of great power.

"I seem to recall," I said, rolling the words around as they came out, "that Sir Caractacus had some quite well-defined views on this subject."

She regarded me with horror. I decided to pour it on a bit.

"What did he say? *I would never defile the immortal name of Bletchley by cheating in so unscrupulous a manner.* Was that it?"

"No, no … er … "

"*Only the most blistering of blistering high-binders would ever entertain that idea for so much as an instant.* Something along those lines, Lady Bletchley?"

"You won't tell him … you can't tell him … "

"Because I'm sure he wouldn't be terribly happy if he found out,"

"No, I say, Mr Stanwick … Jasper … you can't."

"If you'll let me finish … "

My words were quiet, but their effect was immediate and highly gratifying. Lady Bletchley stopped talking.

"As I was saying," I resumed, "I can see how it might be a tad inconvenient for you if Sir Caractacus found out about this … ah, extra-curricular escapade."

I couldn't resist sneaking a glance to see how she was taking it. Rather badly, I noted happily. "I mean, hard to share a house with a blistering high-binder … let alone one who has defiled the family's immortal name and all that."

"Aaarghhh."

"Anyway, should tempers flare, things might come out in the heat of the argument,"

She made a low, animal noise, some way between a whimper and a groan. It was not a thing of beauty.

"And ever since my engagement to Tatty was broken off," I continued, "my temperament has been somewhat … erratic."

There was silence.

"If you catch my drift."

Lady Bletchley looked at me, a model of self-possession once again.

"Am I to gather from your … refreshingly unsubtle

remarks, that, should certain events unfold, you will refrain from mentioning this to anyone."

"You give me Tatty or it's curtains, old girl," I replied, making sure the matter was crystal clear.

She was silent.

"Do we have a deal?"

Chapter 9

At breakfast, the conversation was at a minimum. With the Feather only hours away, an atmosphere of despond and impending humiliation had overtaken those present. But there was one exception: Japper Stanwick was back in full mid-season form. After last night's encounter in the bird loft I was feeling chirpier than at any point since I had first set foot in Daglingworth. In the absence of Gustave, breakfast had drastically regressed back along the evolutionary scale, from the master's *crêpes flambées aux oeufs de caille* to *du canned-tuna sur le pain, à la Compton*. But even so my appetite, having been absent for eighteen hours, had roared into life with a vengeance and I was making short work of the grub.

As I chomped, I mentally reviewed the situation. It was all looking rather mellow. The arctic wastes of Lady Bletchley's icy reserve were undoubtedly starting to thaw, and with them her malign influence over Tatty in re: me.

Sir Caractacus was a man in shock, but would recover in time. So all in all the odds of making it to the altar with Tatty were, I judged, running strongly in my favour. Yet there was one heaping great tsetse fly in the ointment. Adelaide knew about the pigeon-nobbling. And she still had those letters, any one of which could create mayhem chez Bletchley. It was of the utmost importance to recover them as soon as possible.

Murgatroyd and the birds had gone ahead earlier in a great pigeon-transport, to get set up at the race site. Shortly after breakfast, Sir Caractacus and I left in his two-seater, while Compton drove the ladies in the tourer. Sir Caractacus was obviously still brooding deeply on the race, and for fully ten minutes neither of us said a word. When he did speak, it was in an entirely unexpected vein.

"Japper, we have not yet touched upon the proposed match between yourself and Titania."

I nodded, wondering what was to come.

"When you first came to stay," he continued, "I was very much in favour of the marriage. Pigeon man, good family, no slouch at the trencher—what more could one want in a prospective son-in-law? But now I have to tell you … I am not so sure."

I blinked. He ploughed on.

"Indeed, I have severe doubts about the linkage."

My blood ran cold. Could he have discovered my hand in the pigeon mash?

"I am very sorry to hear that, Sir Caractacus. Have I done anything to upset you?"

"Upset me? Goodness, no. Splendid man. No, it's Titania I'm worried about. Japper, the more I look at Titania, the more I see her mother in her. And—without being disloyal to the old girl—that, my friend, is not something any man with good hearing and less than a rhino hide could possibly want." He wheezed with emotion.

"Let me tell you how it was. I wed Pannonica, Polly as she then was, for love. She was everything I was not. Tall, lissom and extremely pretty, yes, if not quite out of the top drawer socially—always makes me laugh when she pulls all that *grande dame* stuff now. But I also loved her for her directness and strength of will. I was rather feckless, and I thought she would put me straight."

He paused to wipe away a tear. "And she did. But over time it all became too much. I found myself becoming someone else. I could not stand it. So I opted out. She became the *grande châtelaine* of Daglingworth, while I became an old buffoon who buried himself in pigeons."

I was frankly astonished by the direction that the conversation had taken.

"I say … "

"And I see myself in you, Japper; daft young testosterone-sodden gadabout that I was. Like me, you are not absolutely overburdened with the grey cells. But you have a gentle soul. You yearn for the easy life. For your sake, and for Titania's,

I am warning you in the friendliest possible way to choose wisely. If you go ahead, I will hugely enjoy having you about the place. But the choices you make now will shape the rest of your existence. As the poet says, 'tis better to have loved and lost than to have spent your whole, ruddy life with her. At your age, you must be. Be! Be! You have … "

"Quite, quite," I said quickly, leaning over and taking hold of the steering wheel, for with his last words he had thrown open his arms, and the car was meandering dangerously into the middle of the road.

"But, dash it all, I mean … Tatty?"

The knight stroked a pensive moustache.

"I am only warning you of an honest man's doubts, m'lad. If you wish to bind her in holy matrimony, I would be the last man to stand in your way. Reflect on it, and follow your heart."

He prattled on, leaving me in ruminative mood.

We arrived at the event an hour or so afterwards. It was an enormous gathering, with countless white tents scattered like sheep across a vast field, and a large marquee at one end. The weather was spectacularly good, which added to the general jollity of the occasion. Like the homing pigeons that he bred, Sir Caractacus made unerringly for the bar in the large marquee, ushering me past various doormen and bouncers. A rather attractive young lady offered me a cocktail. Another one offered me a sausage. I soon began to enjoy myself, especially so now that I held complete power over at least one other member of the Bletchley party. Time to test it out.

"I say," I called loudly through a throng of assembled gentry. "That martini was simply excellent. Could you get me another, Pannonica?"

It arrived shortly thereafter. The cocktail was good, but it was the facial expression that I will treasure for the rest of my life.

This was all exceedingly fine and dandy. But warning bells continued to sound, because Adelaide was nowhere to be seen, and she could at any instant pull the plug on the whole thing. Without Adelaide, I was at risk of a floater of the first magnitude. She still had the letters. And so it was with an uneasy heart that I took my seat at the top table for the President's lunch. To my vast amusement the Bletchleys had been placed directly opposite the Hutchinson-Hineses. Sir Caractacus and Adelaide's father, Lord Algernon, even seemed to be getting on rather well. Tatty and I were seated some way below the salt, but even so I could hear them yelling happily away at each other.

"And then the Countess of Berkshire leant over to him and said, 'You ass, Boko, it's pronounced *quiche*,'" roared Lord Algernon, slapping his knee in joyous abandon.

"Oh stop!" forced out Sir Caractacus, his eyes streaming. "That's just too good. Isn't that the funniest thing you've ever heard?"

But if the menfolk were enjoying each other's company, their respective wives were quickly locked into the social equivalent of graeco-roman wrestling.

"My dearest Cecilia," spat Lady Pannonica, in a tone that would have melted sealing wax. "What a unique dress you are wearing!"

"Yes," her counterpart retorted. "I have often been complimented on it. Apparently I have an instinct for that sort of thing."

"They say instinct is the bastard son of taste, but I never know what that means," continued Lady Pannonica languidly. Lady Cecilia's eyes flashed.

"I don't doubt it. But my own Pannonica, you too look divine. Can that be the same dress you wore last year? I do hope matters are not too straitened between you and Caractacus."

Lady Pannonica was swelling up to deliver what would undoubtedly have been one of the epic putdowns of the season. But at this point Adelaide entered in a short white dress, looking as fresh and beautiful as new-mown hay, and greeted her parents. The moment had passed. Then Adelaide caught sight of me.

"Darling Jasper, don't tell me you're here," she said with utter disingenuousness. "What a joy. May I come and sit next to you?"

I caught sight of Tatty. She wore an expression of absolute loathing.

"I, er, that is to say … "

Before I could anything more, Tatty had placed her hand dangerously high up my thigh.

"Miss Hutchinson-Hines?" she gasped, with the broken, breathless words of one severely winded.

"Do call me Adelaide. It's Titty, isn't it?"

Tatty drew herself a little higher up in her chair. My heart was pounding as never before.

"You may call me Titania. You and Jasper are old friends?"

"No, no," I put in. "We've met a few times."

"*Old* friends," said Adelaide with emphasis.

"You were acquainted at some Book Club, no doubt?"

"Actually, we went to university together," replied Adelaide nonchalantly, as she helped herself to a large slice of roast beef with all the trimmings.

Tatty was now aggressively rubbing my leg, well up the thigh.

"University? Horticulture, perhaps?"

Adelaide looked up. "Metaphysics, as it happens."

"Ah, astrology, how quaint," said Tatty.

"So," Adelaide pressed on. "Which university did you attend?"

Tatty briskly changed the subject.

"I see you are enjoying your meal," she said.

"I have never subscribed to the pathetic attitudes of insecure, self-hating women who seem to believe that, without dieting, life cannot go on," riposted Adelaide in rather heated tones.

"Ah, yes. So I see," Tatty replied, with a little giggle.

There was a moment's pause, as the two women held each other's gaze. I felt like I was stranded in No-Man's Land.

"Call of nature!" I announced loudly, and left at speed.

I took my time coming back, and at last located Adelaide behind the marquee.

"Your girlfriend with the name like a sex game, she really is insufferable isn't she?"

"Well, I … er … "

"Absolutely foul. And *so* overprotective."

"Um … that's a little … "

"Oh, don't pretend you haven't noticed it, Japper. The way she was clasping your leg the entire time was perfectly disgraceful. It's not as though your legs are anything to write home about."

"Well, I say … "

"And her manners! That high-falooting, look-down-my-nose-at-everyone … eeucchh. Anyway, it doesn't matter. The key thing is: how did you get on with that little task I set you?"

I chose my words carefully.

"Ahh … all taken care of."

"Really?"

"Yes."

She gave me a kiss. "Oh Jasper, you are a baa-lamb."

"I hope you're pleased with what you have achieved."

She smirked, and tossed her hair back.

"Actually, to tell you the truth, I really don't care now either way."

I took a step back in disbelief. What was she talking about? What had I put myself through under her instructions?

"Excuse me?" I babbled.

"I'm rather cross at Daddy at the moment. He just downright refused to buy me another pony."

"But, what about your family honour?"

"What about it? Pigeon racing is only a way to get at the Bletchleys. It doesn't exactly carry much interest as a sport."

"But … you … "

"Means to an end, Japper. Bye-ee."

She turned to go back inside, but I cut her off.

"I say, Adelaide … since you have no further use for those letters … could you, er, possibly … "

She extracted the sheaf of papers from her handbag, and handed them over. I pocketed them, relief flooding over me.

"Although you're not very clever, are you, Japper?" she continued.

I looked up.

"How's that?"

"Well, there isn't a signature among them. You ended them all with a squiggle."

I scanned through them feverishly. She was right. The letters were completely untraceable to me. In order to add some element of spice and mystery, I had always signed off with a loopy sort of trademark, sometimes accompanied by the dread words *'your secret admirer'*. The whole thing was for nothing. I could have kicked myself.

"Anyway, *adieu*, Japper," said Adelaide—a touch voluptuously, I felt—and she was gone.

With an hour to go we finally caught up with Murgatroyd. The craggy Scotsman looked like he had a serious case of the medical condition known to science as the screaming heeby-jeebies.

"He didnae eat her food this morning," he confided anxiously. "Summat's seriously wrong."

Long resigned to his fate, Sir Caractacus was unmoved.

"Yes, Dart of Daglingworth is looking a bit off-colour, isn't he," he said, peering into the box where the bird lay. "Decidedly peaky, I should say."

'Decidedly peaky' was the understatement of the century. I'm no expert on pigeons, but it looked to me like the poor thing wouldn't make it out of the starting-basket within ten minutes of the off. It was almost green in colour, and was curled up in the corner emitting the occasional faint squawk. Its breast was conspicuously lacking in puff, while a haggard wing rested on the poor creature's stomach, as if to try to soothe the pain.

"Yes," the sage continued. "But with the CIA spiking the truffle mash, what can we expect? No, Murgatroyd, we must take it on the chin. Patience is a bitter plant, but its fruit is sweet. Cicero? Anyway, he had the right idea."

And he tottered off sadly to take his seat.

I will not bore the reader with a detailed description of the Queen's Feather, the last race of the day; suffice it to say that we went down to ignominious defeat. I recall it vividly: the starting gates opening, the surge of white and grey as thousands of racing pigeons streamed out, wheeled round and swarmed into the sky; and then as we watched them go, our own bird making a tentative leap out of the box and fluttering on the spot for a few moments, before promptly giving up and collapsing. As the pigeon faded, so faded the last vain flicker of hope in Lady Bletchley's eyes. There was a short closing ceremony in which Her Majesty congratulated all involved. We would not know for hours yet which bird had won. But we knew which one had lost. Back in the marquee the Hutchinson-Hineses took special care to come over and commiserate with Sir Caractacus and Lady Pannonica over Dart of Daglingworth's tragic loss of form.

To my surprise Gustave had arrived. He was a little paler and a little thinner than I remembered him, but otherwise seemed to be in good health.

"'Ow was ze start, Sir Caractacoo? *Nous allons gagner?*"

"No," replied the knight sombrely. "We aren't going to win."

"But … " the Frenchman looked around him, anguish on his face. "Our pigeon was … so good … we fed 'er my special truffle mash."

"Yes, and it was the truffle mash that proved her undoing," continued the knight. "Just as it proved to be for us."

"*Monsieur, non!*" interrupted Gustave, emphatically. "I made two batches … I laid one aside for the pigeons … What we ate was the other … "

Sir Caractacus hopped around in anguish.

"What? What on earth are you saying?"

"I would be willing to swear, *monsieur*, that the pigeons were given no – how you say – *altération*."

"But then why the devil did the Dart do so badly?"

For some reason Lady Bletchley had taken a sudden and overwhelming interest in her piece of strawberry shortcake. Then the explanation suddenly struck me. The pigeon had never ingested any of the mysterious powder at all. It was Lady Bletchley who had drugged the pigeon, with her constipation pill. My eyes met hers. She was silently pleading with me.

"Must have been a placebo," I heard Sir Caractacus say somewhere in the background. "That's the only possible reason. Or psychology: the Dart must have heard us doing down his chances, and gone in with the wrong mental attitude."

We Stanwicks are magnanimous in victory. I smiled graciously at Lady Pannonica, and walked off.

"Hello again Japper."

I turned, and found Adelaide at my elbow. She continued to look extremely pretty in her white dress.

"Hello there."

"Having a good time?"

"Splendid. And you?"

"Oh frightfully good. Daddy's terrifically pleased with himself now that he's finally beaten the Bletchleys. He's agreed to get me that new pony. So it all worked out rather well."

There was the sound of someone clearing their throat meaningfully to my right. It was Tatty.

"Could we please have a few moments alone?" she asked rather sharply.

"Suit yourself. See you soon, Jasper," replied Adelaide.

Tatty took my hand, and clasped it.

"Jasper, I have been very tolerant of your behaviour thus far, but the way you were flirting with that … that she-wolf is *very* difficult to endure. There is only so much a self-respecting girl can bear."

She looked up at me with those wide eyes of hers.

"Anyway, that's by and by. The point is this, darling: it's wonderful news. Mama has had a change of heart and given us the go-ahead."

"What?!"

"It's on, Japper, the wedding's on! I think you'll agree she was right to have her doubts concerning your suitability. But, *in spite of this*, I have persuaded her that you are well-meaning. I can come to terms with your weaknesses, Japper, and you can learn. When Mama gave me permission just now, it reminded me that deep down I really am awfully fond of you."

She took a step back and looked at me, a little breathless.

"So, Japper, don't you see what this means? You're not too far beneath me! We can get married after all!"

I regarded her, silhouetted against the afternoon sun. She looked stunning. I had pulled the big one. It was a dream come true.

"No, Tatty," I heard myself say, and she blinked, unable to register what she heard. "I would never defile myself with a girl like you. You and your mother can fuck off."

And with that, I turned and walked away and into a better life.

The End